INDIAN
OCEAN

SOUTHERN
OCEAN

The Orchard Book of

Stories from the Seven Seas

For my niece Georgia, with love,
to guide you on your journey
P.C.

𝕆

For Janet and Steve
S.M.

ORCHARD BOOKS
96 Leonard Street, London EC2A 4RH
Orchard Books Australia
14 Mars Road, Lane Cove, NSW 2066
ISBN 1 85213 929 3
First published in Great Britain 1996
Text © Pomme Clayton 1996
Illustrations © Sheila Moxley 1996
The right of Pomme Clayton to be identified as the author and Sheila Moxley
as the illustrator of this work has been asserted by them in accordance
with the Copyright, Designs and Patents Act, 1988.
A CIP catalogue record for this book is available from the British Library.
Printed in Dubai

The Orchard Book of
Stories from the Seven Seas

Retold by Pomme Clayton

Illustrated by Sheila Moxley

ORCHARD BOOKS

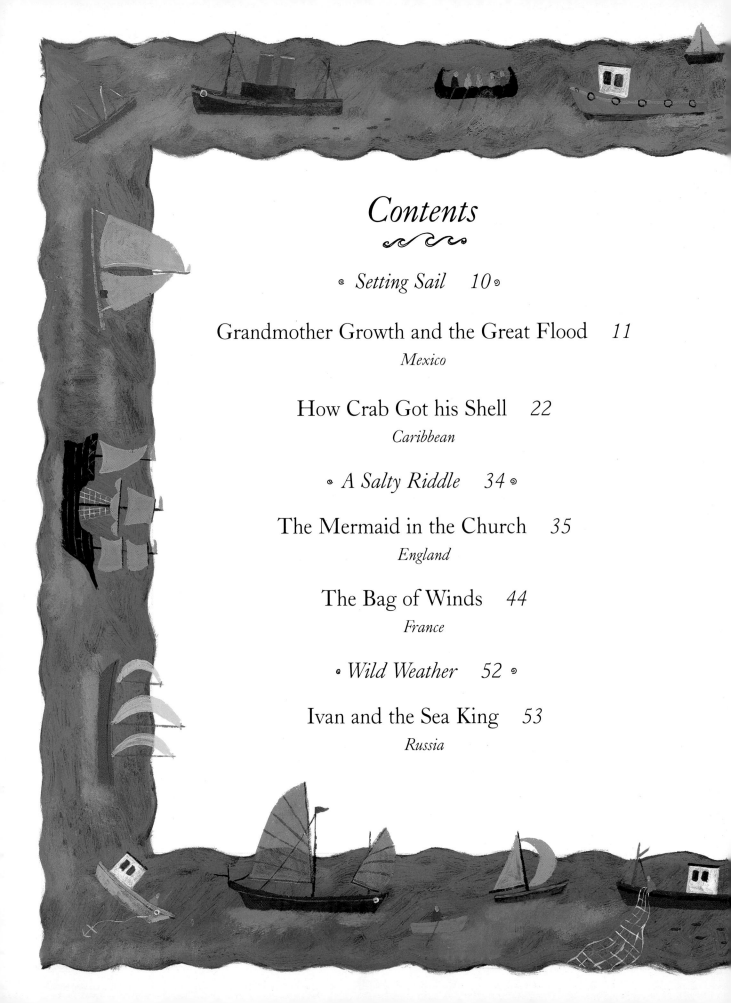

Contents

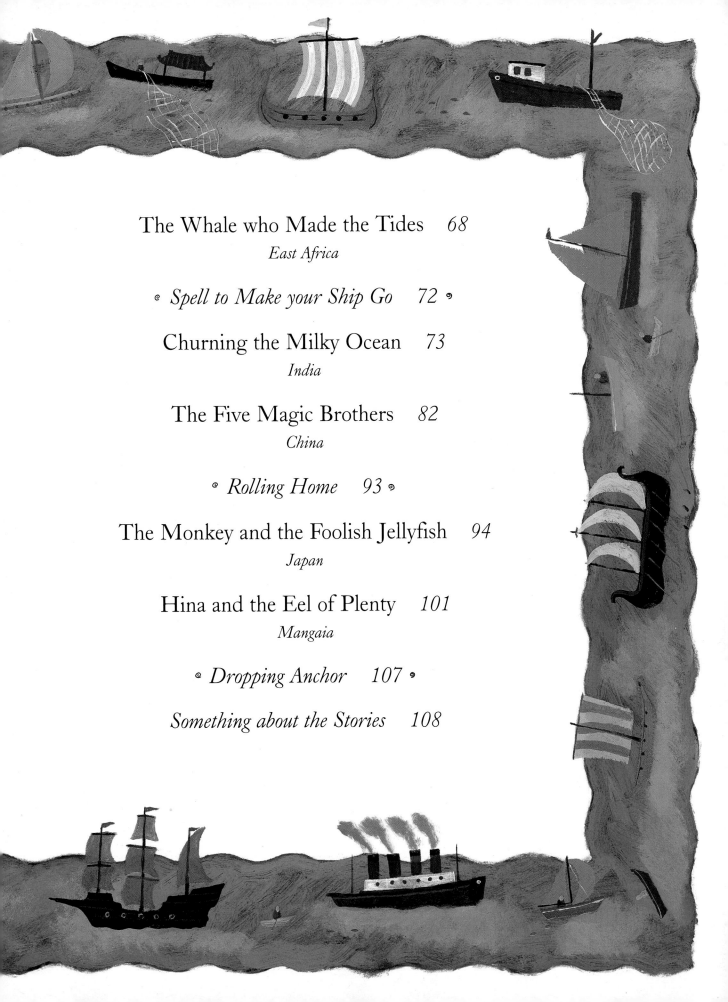

Setting Sail

The one who tells it
to the one who asks to hear it,
gives as a gift
the whole earth and her belt of seas.
Stay with me
and tell me that tale.

Indian saying

GRANDMOTHER GROWTH
AND THE GREAT FLOOD

MEXICO

In the very beginning, there was only one man on earth.
He was called Kauymali, and he lived on top of a wild
mountain in a rancheria – a house made of mud and
stone. He was all alone, except for a little black dog
who kept him company.

Kauymali longed for a friend, for another
human being to talk to. He hoped and prayed
that someone would pass by, but nobody did, for
there was not another living soul on earth.

"Perhaps," thought Kauymali, "if I
grow enough food for a feast, then
somebody might come along!"

So Kauymali set about
growing enough food for a
whole family. He took his
axe and chopped down
some of the pine trees
that surrounded

his rancheria. He cut back a clearing big enough for a field, and he dug
the earth until it was smooth. Then he planted rows of corn, rows of
pumpkin and rows of beans. All the food a family would need to live.

Every day Kauymali went to the field to tend his crops. But there
were no green shoots. He waited, but there were no strong stalks.
The ground was parched and dry like a desert and nothing grew.
Kauymali was very disappointed.

"Oh why won't anything grow?"
he sighed.

Suddenly, there was a gust of wind
and there before him
stood an old, old woman.
It was Grandmother
Growth, the oldest of the
old, who brings new life.
She had a face like a
wrinkled brown berry and
hair like snow white wool.
She wore a rough woven
blanket and she was leaning
on a wooden staff.

Grandmother Growth had heard Kauymali.

"Your crops will not grow, my son," she said shaking her head,
"because the ground is too dry. Crops need water and lots of it! Do as I
say and your field will flourish!"

Grandmother Growth pointed her staff at a twisted fig tree.

"Make a box from that fig tree, about your width and your length."

Kauymali took his axe and cut down the fig tree. He made a box of fig wood, just a little wider and a little longer than himself. Then he made a lid of fig wood that fitted the box perfectly. The wood was so fresh that the box sprouted branches and green leaves!

When the box was finished, Grandmother Growth tapped the ground with her staff and a little embroidered pouch appeared. She filled the pouch with five grains of corn, five pumpkin seeds and five beans. She tapped the ground with her staff a second time and a pumpkin appeared. She peeled a thin slice of pumpkin rind. Then she tapped the ground a third time and a tiny piece of coal appeared. Grandmother Growth blew on the coal and it glowed red-hot with fire. She placed the burning coal on the pumpkin rind and it smouldered safely.

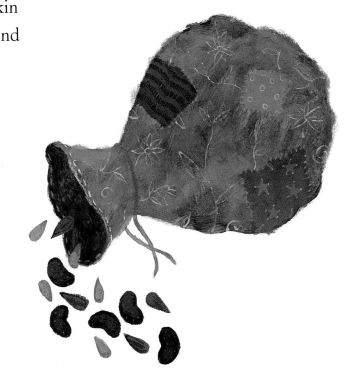

"You will be needing these things when you arrive," she said, handing the pouch of seeds and the pumpkin rind to Kauymali.

"Now into the box with you, and call that dog of yours."

"But where am I going?" asked Kauymali.

"Oh, you'll see when you get there!" said the old woman.

Kauymali whistled, and his little black dog leapt straight into the box. Kauymali followed, and there was just enough room for him to snuggle down with the dog at his feet.

Then Grandmother Growth fitted the fig-tree lid on to the box. Inside the burning coal glowed, filling the box with light.

Grandmother Growth climbed on top of the box and sat down. A parrot, a duck and a macaw swooped down beside her, and perched in the sprouting branches. Then Grandmother Growth pointed her staff at the sky. There was a gush of wind, dark clouds appeared and it began to rain. The rain fell in large drops, splashing and pounding on to the box. The sky turned black and it rained and rained and rained. The rain soaked the dry ground until it was a marsh. There was so much rain, that the ground was awash with water and the fig-tree box began to float. It poured with rain until the whole world was flooded in water.

Inside the box it was warm and safe. Kauymali listened to the drumming of the rain, and as the box rocked from side to side in the swelling waters, he fell asleep. It rained without stopping. It rained for one year, for two years, it rained for three years, for four years. And the box carried Kauymali and the dog, the pouch of seeds and the pumpkin rind, Grandmother Growth and the birds in the branches, over the high seas. They drifted north, south, east and west, to the four farthest points of the world.

Then, in the fifth year, Grandmother Growth pointed her staff at the dark clouds and it stopped raining. The clouds scattered and there was blue sky and hot sun. Drop by drop, the water began to dry up, until a little mountain peak jutted up above the water. Grandmother Growth steered the box with her staff towards the mountain top. But the ground was just thick, slimy mud and they could not land. They had to wait until all the mud had dried up. But the duck could not wait. She dived down into the mud. Her feet got covered in thick clay. The wet mud stuck fast between her toes, and it is still there to this very day –

for ducks have had webbed feet ever since!

After five days the water drained away and the ground was dry at last. Grandmother Growth tapped on the box with her staff.

"We are here, my son."

Kauymali and the dog leapt out of the box. The world was beautiful. Everything was fresh and lush. There were waterfalls and green plants, brightly coloured flowers and the scent of thick pine forests. There were wild crags and sheer ravines and the purple-blue haze of distant mountains. The world was tender and new, like a shining looking glass.

"Plant your seeds, Kauymali," whispered Grandmother Growth. "Now, they will grow. And perhaps, somebody will come along."

Then there was a gush of wind, and Grandmother Growth was gone.

Kauymali took the glowing coal from the pumpkin rind and kindled a fire. Then he set to work. He built a new rancheria of mud and stone, surrounded by storehouses. He cut back a huge clearing and dug the earth until it was smooth. Then he carefully planted the grains of corn, the pumpkin seeds and the beans.

It was not long before green shoots burst from the soil. The earth was rich and damp and everything grew. The corn was long and golden, the pumpkins swelled, and the beans were fat and juicy. Kauymali filled his storehouses with tasty crops. There was more than enough food for a family! Kauymali was sure that somebody would come soon. But nobody did. There was still not another living soul on earth.

Then one day, when Kauymali was returning from his field, he smelt the warm scent of baking coming from his rancheria. Kauymali went inside and there by the fire was a freshly baked tortilla – his favourite food! Kauymali gobbled up the little pancake. It was just right, hot and floury on the outside, and soft and stuffed with spicy sauce on the inside!

"Who left this tortilla for me?" he wondered. "It must have been a present from Grandmother Growth."

The next day there was another tortilla by the fire. And it was just as good as the first. But on the third day, when there was a third tortilla, Kauymali thought, "Grandmother Growth would not leave me three tortillas. Somebody else must be making them for me and I am going to find out exactly who it is!"

So the next morning Kauymali took his blanket, hat and digging tools and said in a very loud voice, in case somebody was listening, "I'm just off to work in the field!"

Then, instead of going out, he hid behind the door. He did not have to wait long, for into the house trotted his own little black dog. Kauymali watched. The dog dug her claws into her fur and there was a ripping and a tearing sound. The little black dog peeled off her skin, as if she was taking off a fur coat, and out stepped a graceful girl! She had long black hair and shining black eyes, and she was just about the same age as Kauymali. The girl went over to the fire and put a handful of ground corn into a pot of warm water. Then she stirred the pot to make the batter for tortillas.

Kauymali was amazed.

"A FRIEND!" he shouted joyfully, leaping out from behind the door, "YOU HAVE ARRIVED AT LAST!"

Kauymali was so happy to see another human being, he did not want to lose her ever again. So he bent down, picked up the black dog's skin and threw it on to the fire. The dog's skin burst into flames. But as the skin burnt, the girl began to howl with pain. She was burning. The girl was covered in terrible burns from head to foot.

Kauymali rushed over to the pot of warm corn water. He picked it up and dashed the water over the girl's burnt body. As the corn water touched her sore skin, all the burns vanished and her skin was completely healed. There was not a mark on her body.

"Thank you, Kauymali," she whispered. "You have broken the spell. Now I can be a human being at last!"

Then Kauymali and his new friend cooked tortillas. They sat by the fire, and they ate and they talked and they laughed, as if it had never been any other way. And in time they had a family – and there was more than enough food for everyone!

And their children had children, who had children who had children, who populated the whole of Mexico. And their children are the Huichol people of Mexico. They still remember Kauymali and his wife, the little black dog – and how they survived the great flood in a fig-tree box. And to this day they say that the best cure for a burn is to soothe it with warm corn water.

HOW CRAB
GOT HIS SHELL

CARIBBEAN

Once there was an old Witch who lived in a cave beside the sea. The
Witch was a powerful sorceress. She could conjure up sunshine or
storms, turn lead into gold or humans into animals, and she knew the
dark spell of invisibility. She did *not* use her magic kindly.

All the Witch's power was embedded in her name. If anyone spoke her name out loud, her magic would disappear for ever. But nobody knew the Witch's name. Except for her three children – Starfish, Shrimp and Crab. And they were forbidden, on pain of death, to tell anyone her secret name.

One day the Witch went down to the edge of the sea, to the rock pool where she kept her children.

"Crab," she ordered, "I need a servant to do all my cooking and cleaning. Go to market and get me a girl. If she works for me for a week, she can have half the food on my table, half the clothes in my cupboard and half the gold in my purse. But only if she can guess my name, and guess it right!"

At that the Witch threw back her head and cackled with laughter.

"But nobody can guess my name, because nobody knows it! So I will get all the work, for nothing."

Then the Witch pointed her bony finger at Starfish, Shrimp and Crab.

"Nobody knows my name except for you. And if you tell anyone, you know what will happen. So don't even think about it!"

Now Crab was a bit different from how crabs are today. He did not have a shell. He just had firm pink flesh on his back. Crab clambered out of the pool and covered his tender back with a large leaf, to protect him from the sun and from hungry birds. Then he crawled sideways to the village.

When Crab got to market he called out in his loudest voice, "If there are any girls who want to work for the Witch for a week, they can have half the food on her table, half the clothes in her cupboard, and half the gold in her purse. But only if they can guess her name, and guess it right."

A young girl followed Crab, sideways, back to the Witch's cave. The Witch was delighted to see her and set her to work at once. The girl did the cooking and cleaned the cave, polished the Witch's pointed shoes and dusted her books of spells. The girl worked hard. She worked without stopping. Then at the end of the week the Witch said, "Right girl, you have three guesses. What's my name?"

The girl thought about all the witches in all the stories that she had heard.

"Ummm... Morgan Le Fay?" she said.

"No," sneered the Witch, "King Arthur's enchantress was nothing but a fairy!"

"Baba Yaga?"

"No, that's my sister in Russia!"

"Winnie?"

"Certainly not, he's a bear!" shouted the Witch. "Wrong, wrong, wrong!"

The girl began to cry. At once the Witch picked up a calabash, a hollowed-out pumpkin, and held it under the girl's chin. The girl's tears rolled down her cheeks and plopped straight into the calabash.

"Waste not want not!" cried the Witch.

When the girl had gone, the Witch counted up the gold in her purse, looked at the tidy cave and laughed at all the hard work she had got for nothing.

It wasn't long before another girl came to work for the Witch. She worked hard, she worked without stopping. And at the end of the week the Witch said, "Right girl, three guesses. What's my name?"

"Mother Holle?"

"No, she lives under the ground in Germany."

"Hecate?"

"Never, she's much too helpful."

"Kali?"

"No, she's my second cousin in India. But I like her necklace of skulls. Wrong, wrong, wrong!"

The girl began to cry and the Witch caught all her tears in the calabash.

Every week a different girl came and worked for the Witch. But not one of them could guess her secret name. Until, waste not want not, the Witch had caught one hundred girls' tears in her calabash.

Then the girls stopped coming. Nobody wanted to work for

nothing. The cave got very dirty. So the Witch sent Crab off to market to find a new servant.

Crab put a leaf on his back and crawled sideways to the village. He shouted in his loudest voice, "If there are any girls who want to work for the Witch for a week, they can have half the food on her table, half the clothes in her cupboard, and half the gold in her purse. But only if they can guess her name, and guess it right."

All the girls shook their heads. Nobody wanted to work for the Witch.

But Anansi the Spider was sunning himself in a tree and he heard everything. He fanned himself lazily. "Half the food... yum yum. Half the clothes... yes

please. Half the gold... absolutely! All I have to do is guess that stupid old Witch's name." Anansi the Spider spun a thread and dropped out of the tree. He touched the ground and turned into a man.

"The only thing is," he muttered, "I have to disguise myself as a girl!"

So Anansi went to market and bought a little girl's dress. He squeezed himself into it. The sleeves were too tight and it did not cover his knees. He struggled into white socks and a dainty pair of patent leather shoes. He put on a straw hat and pulled the brim down over his face.

Anansi set off to the Witch's cave. He was so busy thinking about all the gold he would get, he quite forgot about all the work he would have to do.

"Good day, Mrs Witch," he said in a little girl's voice, "I am your new servant."

The Witch was so glad to see another girl, she did not look too closely at Anansi. She pointed to a huge pile of washing in the corner of the cave.

"You can start with that!" she instructed.

Anansi took the washing down to the rock pool.

WASH
WHITE

And as he splashed about in the water, he saw Starfish, Shrimp and Crab.

"They must be the Witch's children," he thought. "I bet they know her name." So he fumbled in his pockets and found a few fluffy crumbs. And he fed the crumbs to Starfish, Shrimp and Crab.

"Oh, Mr Crab!" said Anansi in his sweetest little girl voice. "You are so big and handsome."

"Why thank you, little girl," blushed Crab. Nobody had called him handsome before. "And you are very sweet too."

"If ever I was in trouble, Mr Crab," lisped Anansi, "I know a big handsome crab like you would help a sweet little girl like me."

"Just ask," boasted Crab.

"Any time?" asked Anansi.

"Any time," said Crab.

Anansi finished the washing and went back to the Witch's cave. As soon as one job was finished, another one had begun. Anansi had never worked so hard in his whole life. He worked without stopping. But whenever he felt tired, he just thought about the Witch's gold.

At last it was the end of the week and the Witch said, "Right girl, three guesses. What's my name?"

"Oh, Mistress Witch," sighed Anansi, "I have been working so hard, I haven't thought of any names. Can I have five minutes to put my thinking cap on?"

"Well, you'd better put it on fast, your time is running out. Hurry up!" cried the Witch. Then she smiled to herself and greedily counted her gold.

"This girl hasn't got a clue," she mumbled. "That's another week's work for nothing!"

Anansi rushed down to the rock pool. He rubbed his eyes red with

salty water to make it look as if he'd been crying. Then he sobbed in a
loud voice, "Oh dear, oh dear, oh dear!"

Crab poked his head out of the water.

"What's the matter, little girl?"

"I've worked for the Witch all week and I won't get paid a penny
unless I can guess her name. And I don't know any names."

Crab was very soft hearted and he hated seeing the little girl cry.

"I said I would help you any time," said Crab kindly, "and I will keep
my word. I will tell you the Witch's name. But you must promise not to
tell her who told you."

Anansi nodded and dried his pretend tears. Crab climbed out of the
pool and whispered to Anansi, behind his claw, the Witch's secret magic
name.

"Thank you!" cried Anansi and ran back to the cave.

"Well, girl, what's my name?" asked the Witch.

"Old Hag?" said Anansi.

"No, and don't be rude."

"Spindle-shanks?"

"Certainly not, my legs are very shapely!"

The Witch was just reaching for her calabash, when Anansi shouted, "Your name is – IN THE STORM COFFIN ON YOUR BACK!"

In an instant, all the Witch's magic power drained out of her body, away through her pointy shoes and disappeared for ever!

Anansi whipped out a large sack from his pocket. And he swept all the food from the table, all the clothes from the cupboard, and all the gold from the purse, into the sack.

"Anansi guessed your name!" he cried, throwing off the hat and kicking off the shoes. "Anansi the Spider guessed your name," he laughed, ripping off the dress. Then he slung the sack full of goodies over his shoulder and ran off.

The Witch blazed with rage. She had lost all her magic, all her food, all her clothes and all her money. The only thing she had left was her calabash full of girls' tears.

"Someone has told him my name," she shrieked. "And I am going to find out just who it was."

The Witch snatched up the calabash, rushed to the rock pool and lined her children up in a row.

"Starfish," she growled, "did you tell my name?"

"No, miss," said Starfish.

"Shrimp, did you tell my name?"

"No, miss," said Shrimp.

"Crab, did you tell my name?"

Crab looked sideways and said nothing.

"Crab," snarled the Witch, "did you tell my name?"

"Yes," said Crab. "It was me."

"You told my name?" roared the Witch, plunging into the rock pool. Crab scuttled sideways.

"Yes," he cried. "It was me."

The Witch was so furious she lifted up the calabash and threw it at Crab. The calabash landed upside down on Crab's back. And all the girls' tears made the calabash stick fast.

Suddenly Crab felt different. With the magic calabash stuck to his back, he felt big and strong and handsome. In fact, he felt just like a crab!

"Yes, IN THE STORM COFFIN ON YOUR BACK!" Crab shouted, "IT IS ME!"

Crab opened up his mouth and he ate up the Witch, name and all. And that was the end of her.

And that is how Crab got his shell. And crabs have had shells ever since.

Anansi made it so!

A Salty Riddle

Creaking, cracking, hard,

Flesh inside its bones,

Eyes upon its back,

Hands that can crush stones!

What is it?

Old Gaelic

THE MERMAID IN THE CHURCH

ENGLAND

Many years ago, in a little fishing village on the far tip of Cornwall,
lived Squire Trewella and his wife and their handsome young son
Mathey. Now Mathey had a good singing voice and he sang in the
church choir. And every Sunday all the fishermen and their families
would go to church to hear Mathey sing.

One Sunday Mathey was sitting in the choir stalls, listening to the
Priest read from the Bible, when he heard a flip-flapping sound.
Something flip-flapped up the church path, flip-flapped
through the church porch and flip-flapped down the aisle.

It was a mermaid! She was a woman from the waist up, but from the waist down she had a gleaming fish's tail. Her skin was pale green, her hair golden, and her fingers were webbed like a water bird's.

The Mermaid flip-flapped down the aisle and sat in the front pew. Everyone was astonished, except for the Priest who just carried on reading. The Mermaid combed her hair with a fishbone comb and gazed at herself in a pearly mirror. When the choir began to sing, the Mermaid opened her mouth and joined in. Her voice did not sound human. It sounded like water murmuring and wind whistling, like a colony of sea-birds calling and silver bells chiming under the sea. When all the hymns were sung, the Mermaid flip-flapped out of the church and splashed into the sea.

As soon as the service was over, the congregation gathered outside the church and began to talk.

"It just isn't right, a mermaid coming into a church."

"Dripping water everywhere!"

"She's only half human with that fish's tail!"

"And half naked too!"

But the Priest said firmly, "The church is God's house. It is open to every living thing, whether they have tails or wings, fins or legs. And as

for half human, well Jesus was half human, for he was the Son of God. If the Mermaid wants to come into the church, I'm not going to stop her."

Only one other person agreed with the Priest, and that was Mathey Trewella. But he said nothing, for he thought that the Mermaid was the loveliest creature that he'd ever seen, with the sweetest voice that he'd ever heard. Mathey could hardly wait for next Sunday!

The week dragged by. And when Sunday finally came, Mathey went to church early, hoping that he would see the Mermaid again.

After the first hymn he heard the flip-flapping sound, as the Mermaid flip-flapped up the church path, flip-flapped through the church porch, flip-flapped down the aisle and sat in the front pew. Mathey could hardly take his eyes off her. He watched her comb her hair with the bony comb and gaze at herself in the pearly mirror and he listened spellbound to her haunting song. When the Mermaid flip-flapped out of the church and splashed into the sea, Mathey had to summon up all his strength to stop himself from racing after her and plunging into the waves.

At the end of the service hullabaloo broke loose. The congregation didn't even wait to get outside the church, they all started to shout at once.

"We're being bewitched!"

"She's casting spells on us all!"

"We'll be lured under the tide!"

But the Priest said very firmly, "This is God's house and it is open to all. No one will shut the Mermaid out." And he propped open the church door with a large stone.

But still Mathey said nothing – for he was in love. Well, two strong young fishermen, Tom and John, disagreed with the Priest. They got talking and decided that if the Priest wasn't going to put a stop to the Mermaid, they would. They planned to catch her in a net. Then they could sell her, or put her on show, or cut her up for mermaid steaks.

So early next Sunday morning, before anyone was about, Tom and John rigged up a net over the church door, with a rope that dangled to the ground. The Mermaid would trip over the rope, then the net would drop on top of her and she would be theirs!

Mathey put on his best suit of clothes and polished his shoes, for he longed to see the Mermaid again. He was so excited, he didn't notice the odd bit of rope in the church porch. He rushed to the choir stalls and waited. As soon as he heard the flip-flapping sound, his heart skipped a beat. The Mermaid flip-flapped up the church path and flip-flapped through the church porch. Mathey waited with bated breath. But the flip-flapping sound stopped. He waited and waited, but there was no Mermaid. So, as soon as everyone had closed their eyes to pray, Mathey crept down the aisle and out of the church. And what a sight met his eyes! For there in the porch was the Mermaid caught in a net, weeping and struggling to get free. At once Mathey picked her up in his arms and carried her down to the sea.

At the end of the service Tom and John raced to the porch to examine their catch, but there was no Mermaid to be seen. And no net. And no Mathey.

Squire Trewella and his wife waited for their son to come home for Sunday lunch, but he didn't arrive. That afternoon a search party was called and everyone began to look for Mathey. They scoured the caves and along the cliffs, they searched the harbour and inside all the boats, but there was no sign of him. The search went on for a week, until everyone sadly agreed that Mathey must have been drowned at sea, lured into the water by the Mermaid's song. A gravestone was placed in the churchyard with 'Matthew Trewella' inscribed upon it, but his body was never found.

Many years passed. Squire Trewella and his wife grew old and died and were buried beside their son's empty grave. The Priest was very old, and Tom and John both had grey hair and grandchildren.

One day old Tom and John were out fishing together in their little rowing boat. They let down their anchor and were just about to cast their nets, when they heard a splash. They looked over the side of the boat and there, in the water, was a face. It was a woman with pale green skin and golden hair floating about her and a shining fish's tail. It was the Mermaid! Tom and John were terrified.

"Good sirs," said the Mermaid sweetly, "you have dropped your anchor right across my front door. Would you be so kind as to haul it up, so that I can get inside my house and give my children their tea?"

Tom and John were struck dumb with terror. They quickly pulled up the anchor before the Mermaid could lure them under the tide. Then they heard a second splash and their hearts froze. They looked over the side of the boat and this time they saw a Merman! He was young and strong and very handsome. He had golden hair and a glittering fish's tail. And he looked rather familiar.

"Hello Grandads!" said the Merman.

Tom and John stared – it was Matthew Trewella. And he didn't look a day older than when they last saw him fifty years ago!

"Thank you for helping my wife," said Mathey. "Give my regards to the Priest. Tell him all is well down here with my wife and children under the waves."

Then *splash*! and Mathey was gone.

The two old fishermen rowed with their feeble arms, as fast as they could, back to the harbour. Then they ran on their feeble legs, as fast as they could, up the hill to the church.

"We saw Mathey Trewella!" they shouted breathlessly. "He is alive and living under the sea with the Mermaid. He has a fish's tail, and he doesn't look a day older than he did fifty years ago!"

The old Priest listened and shook his head. "That's what happens," he said, "if you keep anyone, whoever they are, out of the church."

The Priest took a hammer and chisel and began to carve a figure on the front pew. He carved a picture of the Mermaid, with long hair and a fish's tail, a bony comb in one hand and a pearly mirror in the other and her mouth open singing.

"But now," said the Priest, "the Mermaid is in the church and no one will ever shut her out."

Every Sunday after that the congregation looked at the Mermaid. But when Tom and John looked at her, they felt old and feeble, and secretly wished they were fifty years younger and living with the loveliest wife under the waves.

The carving of the Mermaid is still in the church to this very day. And on a clear night, when the sea is calm, if you listen carefully, you might just hear Mathey and the Mermaid singing.

THE BAG OF WINDS

FRANCE

When the world was first made, there was no wind. No wind at all. The wind did not blow over land or sea. There was no wind to rustle the leaves or whip up the waves. There was no wind to blow away rain clouds or cool down a hot day. There was not even a ripple on the surface of the water. The sea was as still as glass. And in those days, if you wanted to travel by boat, you had to row, and it was back-breaking work.

Now, there was one sea captain who was fed up with rowing everywhere. He had heard that somewhere there was a cave and in that cave lived the winds. And these winds were so strong they could make a ship move! The Captain thought that if he could find the cave and set the winds free, then he would put an end to rowing – for good.

So the Captain set off over a lonely cliff top, to ask the Fishwife if she knew anything about the winds. The Fishwife sold fish in the streets, but her real trade was in tongue wagging. She knew all the gossip and tales of the town, and many charms and spells besides. If the Fishwife didn't know about the winds, then nobody would. The Captain knocked on her cottage door, and a wrinkled old woman, stinking of fish, appeared.

"Come inside, Captain," she croaked. "What can I do for you?"

"I want to find the winds," said the Captain, "and set them free. Do you know where they are?"

"That's what you want, is it?" muttered the Fishwife. "Well, it's a dangerous task. The winds live far up north, in the Country of the Winds. It will be a long journey, and you will need a good ship – fitted with sails."

"Whatever it takes," cried the Captain. "I'm going there!"

"But that's only the beginning, bold Captain," said the Fishwife, sucking her teeth. "The winds are wild and you will have to tame them."

And the Fishwife reached into her apron pocket and pulled out a little wooden pipe.

"Play this pipe and the winds will grow calm. Tie them up in a strong bag and nail the bag to the mast of your ship. Then let the gentle west wind out of the bag and the wind will fill your sails and waft you home.

But whatever you do, don't let any other winds out of the bag until you are safely in harbour."

The Fishwife gave the Captain the little pipe. "And good luck to you," she said, shaking her head.

The Captain walked into town, with the pipe in his pocket, and hired twenty strapping sturdy men to be his crew. He offered each man a bag of gold at the end of the voyage, but he did not tell them where they were going. He fitted a ship with a strong mast and twenty pairs of oars. He had three large sails stitched from canvas, and he made a bag from the toughest ox-hide. He bought kegs of beer and a ton of ship's biscuits to keep the crew going. Then he turned his ship towards the north.

The crew pulled at the oars night and day. And they slowly made their way across the smooth, still water. At first it was hot, and the crew sweated and panted with the effort of rowing. But the further north they rowed, the cooler it became. They rowed north and it grew bitterly, bitterly cold. They rowed north and there were icebergs floating in the

sea and sheer cliffs of snow towering above them. They rowed so far
north that the sea froze and they could row no more.

The ship ran aground beside a cave made of ice. From the cave came
a wild roaring and moaning sound, so terrible that even the strapping,
sturdy crew shuddered. They had reached the Country of the Winds.

The Captain put the ox-hide bag under his arm and tapped his pocket
to make sure the pipe was still there. Then, leaving the crew to guard the
boat, he climbed into the cave.

Suddenly, he was hit by something, something he could not see. It
was so strong it nearly knocked him over and so angry it nearly ripped
the coat from his back. It was the winds! The Captain turned up his
collar and peered about the cave. He could just make out the faint
outlines of eight creatures, ghostly white with great wings.

They were the eight winds. And they were flying round and round
the cave sucking in air and blowing it out. Some of the winds were old
with trailing beards, some were young and forceful, others were bold and
blasting, one was gentle and balmy. The winds swirled and swooped
around each other, blowing hot and cold, wailing and whistling.

The Captain pulled the wooden pipe from his pocket, put it to his lips and began to play. The pipe had a sweet clear tone and the sound soared around the cave. The winds stopped howling and listened. The pipe soothed them and, one by one, they floated softly to the ground and lay at the Captain's feet. Quickly the Captain opened the neck of the bag and swept all eight winds inside. Then he tied up the bag with a stout knot, carried it back to the ship and nailed it to the mast.

"Men," he warned, "you touch this bag on pain of death!"

The Captain ordered his crew to hoist the sails. The crew had never seen sails before, and they heaved and pulled the stiff canvas up the mast in silence. Then the Captain opened the bag, just a tiny bit, and caught the gentle west wind in his fist. He closed the bag swiftly and let the wind loose. The sweet west wind blew softly. The sails filled with air, and the ship began to move across the water by the sheer power of the wind. The crew was amazed! The huge sails billowed and the ship sped over the sea. All the crew had to do was steer. So they took it in turns to guide the helm, while the rest of the crew sat back and enjoyed the ride. They sang sea-shanties, told stories and dozed, and the west wind blew them safely home.

But the youngest member of the crew, the cabin boy, could not take his eyes off the strange bag nailed to the mast. There was something inside it, alive and kicking and struggling to get out. The cabin boy longed to know what it was. He looked about the deck, the crew were all busy or asleep, and he thought to himself, "No one will notice if I take a peep".

So he crept up to the mast, untied the knot, opened the neck of the bag and looked inside. Suddenly, there was a great rush and something white like a ghost burst out of the bag. The cabin boy was terrified and he quickly tied up the knot. But it was too late, for he had let out the

terrible south-west wind. Instantly the south-west wind
filled his cheeks with air and began to blow with all his
might. He roared and bellowed and blew up a gale.
He whipped up huge waves and water washed over
the side of the boat. The south-west wind blew so
hard that the ship was lifted right up into the air. A
whirlwind spun the ship round and round, then a great gust
of wind dashed the ship down on to a rock. The ship smashed
into a thousand pieces. The crew and the Captain and the cabin
boy were all swept into the cold water and drowned.

As the boat broke apart, the bag split open and out flew the
other winds. Now the eight winds were free and that night,
there was the first storm at sea. It was ugly weather and many
boats were wrecked. The eight winds blew their way
across the whole world. And they are still blowing to
this very day. For no one can get the winds back
into the bag.

Ever since then, a ship's crew have been called sailors –
after the sails they use to trap the wind. All sailors wear
sou'westers, oil-skin hats and coats, to protect them from
the terrible south-west wind. And sometimes, when
the sea is calm and there is no wind, sailors whistle
for the wind. But they must be careful and whistle
sweetly – for they never know which wind is
going to come. And they might get more
than they bargained for.

Wild Weather

When the wind is in the east,
   it's neither good for man nor beast.
When the wind is in the north,
   the skilful fisher goes not forth.
When the wind is in the south,
   it blows the bait in the fishes' mouth.
But when the wind is in the west,
   then it's at the very best!

Old English saying

IVAN
AND THE
SEA KING

RUSSIA

Once upon a time, on the shores of the Black Sea, there lived a wealthy merchant and his three sons. The merchant owned a fleet of ships and traded goods throughout Russia. His two eldest sons worked with him, unloading and selling the cargo. But his youngest son, Ivan, spent all day at the inn drinking vodka. And if he wasn't drinking vodka, he was sleeping!

The older boys thought this was very unfair.

"Why should we do all the work?" they complained. "While Ivan does nothing."

One day, down at the harbour, the merchant gave the two older boys a fine ship each. The eldest son's ship was loaded with a cargo of crisp linen. And the second son's ship was loaded with a cargo of delicate tea.

"Thank you for your help, my boys," said the merchant. "Go and make your fortunes."

But Ivan got nothing. He watched his brothers sail away, until their ships were just specks on the horizon. Then he turned to his father and begged, "Can I have a ship and a cargo?"

The merchant laughed. "Ivan, if I give you a cargo, you'll drink it

53

all away."

"Oh please, Father, just a small ship. Then I can make my fortune too."

So the merchant gave Ivan a ship. A very small ship. With rotting timbers and ragged sails and a crew of ancient sailors – crusty old sea dogs. And as for a cargo, there was none. Ivan bid his father goodbye and set sail towards his fortune.

The small ship coasted with the wind, while Ivan drank grog with the old sea dogs. But when the drink ran out, the sailors began to get grumpy. Ivan thought he'd better fill their stomachs to quieten their tempers. So he cast his fishing net overboard. When the net felt heavy he hauled it in and slung it on to the deck. There, struggling inside the net, was a golden octopus!

"I can sell you for a handsome price!" chuckled Ivan.

But the octopus cried out, "Please don't kill me. I am a prince, the son of the great Sea King Chudo Yudo. Let me go and my father will bless you."

Ivan looked longingly at the golden octopus. He would never catch another one like it, and what use was a blessing anyway? He was just about to kill the octopus, when he remembered his own father. How sad he would be if he never saw his father again. Ivan picked up the octopus and flung it overboard.

Suddenly there was a rumbling sound and the sea began to swell. It was as if the very bottom of the ocean was coming to the top. Out of the depths rose a glittering throne, and sitting on the throne was the great Sea King Chudo Yudo. And he was huge! Half man and half octopus, with curling tentacles and a long grey beard, rich red gown and a golden crown on his head.

"As you helped my son," boomed the Sea King, "I will help you!"

He reached under his throne and pulled out a golden dish. "Fill this dish with sea water and leave it on the deck in the midday sun."

Then there was a rumbling and a bubbling, and the Sea King sank down under the waves.

Ivan filled the dish with sea water and placed it on the deck. The hot midday sun beat down and the water dried up. All that was left was a thin film of white powder lining the bottom of the dish. Ivan dipped his finger into the powder and licked it.

"Salt!" he cried. "The Sea King has shown me how to make salt!"

At once, Ivan and the old sea dogs filled pans and pails with sea water and put them on the deck to dry. They worked hard filling pails and scraping out the crystals of salt. Until, after many days, the ship was overflowing with a cargo of the finest salt.

"We won't have any trouble selling this," cried Ivan. "Everyone wants salt!"

Now Ivan sailed! He sailed with the wind and he sailed against the wind, to the city of the Tsar, King of Russia.

When they arrived at port, Ivan put a handful of salt into a little bag.

"My crew," he instructed, "guard the ship well. I'm going to the Tsar to ask for permission to trade." And he put the bag of salt into his pocket.

Ivan was shown into the royal throne room. There was the Tsar and the Tsarina, and sitting between them on a golden footstool was their daughter the Tsarevna. Ivan bowed to the Tsar, and he secretly thought that the Tsarevna was the loveliest maiden he'd ever seen.

"Your Majesty," he said, "I am a merchant and I ask permission to trade in your city."

"What are you trading?" enquired the Tsar.

"Salt," said Ivan.

"Salt?" puzzled the Tsar "What is that?"

Ivan pulled the bag out of his pocket and poured a little salt into the palm of his hand.

"You sprinkle it on your food," he said. "It tastes delicious!" And he offered the Tsar some salt. The Tsar dipped in his finger and licked it.

"UGGGH!" he spluttered. "It tastes disgusting! No one will buy that in my kingdom."

And Ivan was marched out of the palace.

Ivan was very downcast. "Someone must eat salt round here," he thought. "I'm going to find out!"

He went straight to the palace kitchens and begged for a glass of water. The chief cook took him inside and sat him by a roaring fire. Ivan sipped his water, then closed his eyes and pretended to go to sleep. But he peeped out from under his half-closed eyelashes and watched. The cooks were roasting, baking, stewing, frying, stirring and pouring. But no one was concerned with salting. Ivan waited until all the cooks were out of the kitchen. Then he went up to each pot and pan, and put a pinch of salt into every dish.

When the meal was served, the first course was the Tsar's favourite beetroot soup, and it tasted good. The Tsar smacked his lips, the Tsarina dabbed hers, and the Tsarevna licked hers, and they all had seconds! Then came the meat, it tasted excellent and they all had thirds! Then came a mountain of cakes that tasted divine. When the meal was finally over the Tsar called for the chief cook.

"I've never tasted such a delicious meal in all my born days," relished the Tsar, patting his stomach. "What did you do?"

"Your Majesty," replied the cook, "we cooked it in exactly the same way as we always do."

"Nothing different?" asked the Tsar.

"Nothing – except for a merchant who sat by the fire sipping a glass of water."

"Bring me the merchant," ordered the Tsar.

Ivan bowed before the Tsar a second time.

"Oh! It's you," frowned the Tsar. "Did you put anything in the food?"

"Just a sprinkling of salt," said Ivan.

"You mean that terrible tasting powder?"

"Yes, Your Majesty."

"Well I never!" cried the Tsar. "It made the soup soupier, the meat meatier, the vegetables vegetablier and the cake cakeier. I will buy all the salt you have. How much do you want for it!"

"A bag of gold for each bag of salt," said Ivan quickly.

"Done!" cried the Tsar.

The sailors spent all day stuffing salt into bags. And all the next day carrying salt up to the palace. And all the day after that carrying gold down to the ship.

The maiden Tsarevna sat by her window and watched everything. She thought that Ivan was the cleverest man she'd ever met. And when Ivan bowed before the Tsar for the last time, she said sweetly, "Father, please can I go and look at Ivan's ship?"

The Tsar agreed, so Ivan took the Tsarevna by the hand and led her down to the harbour.

"It is only a small ship," he said, helping her aboard.

But the Tsarevna danced across the deck, admiring everything.

"What are those?" she asked, pointing at the rags hanging from the mast.

"The sails!" replied Ivan proudly. "Hoist the sails for the Tsarevna!" he called, and the old sea dogs hoisted the sails.

"But why aren't we moving?"she cried.

"Because of the anchor," answered Ivan.

"What's an anchor?"

"Weigh the anchor for the Tsarevna," shouted Ivan, and the old sea dogs hauled up the anchor. As the Tsarevna examined the anchor, the sails filled with wind and the ship lurched out of the harbour. The Tsarevna turned to Ivan and laughed. And the further out to sea they sailed, the happier she became!

"Oh, Ivan!" she sighed. "I could not bear to be without you."

Ivan and the Tsarevna sat down on a pile of gold and talked. Their talking turned to laughing, their laughing to kissing and in their kissing they fell in love. They were just planning their wedding, when Ivan saw two fine ships on the horizon. It was his brothers! Ivan steered his ship alongside theirs and invited them both aboard.

When the two brothers saw Ivan's gold, they could hardly believe their eyes. And when they met the Tsarevna, their eyes nearly popped out of their heads.

"It just isn't fair," they grumbled to each other. "We do all the work, and Ivan gets the reward."

The two brothers were overcome with jealousy, and they hatched a terrible plan.

That night, when Ivan was keeping watch on deck, his brothers leapt upon him, bound a heavy weight to his feet and hurled him overboard.

"Now!" cried the eldest brother. "I will have the Tsarevna and you can have the gold!" And the two brothers shook hands greedily and sailed home as fast as they could.

Ivan sank like a stone, dragged down by the heavy weight. He sank deeper and deeper under the sea, and he began to drown. Suddenly, a long tentacle wrapped itself around Ivan's waist, gripped him tight and lifted him up through the water.

"As you helped my son, I will help you," boomed a voice.

It was Chudo Yudo, King of the Sea! He swept Ivan out of the water and placed him safely on a rock. Ivan coughed and spluttered and gasped for air, then he told the Sea King the whole story.

"Well," rumbled the Sea King, "we might just get to the church in time!"

And he lifted Ivan high up on to his shoulders. Then he set off with giant strides, splashing and rushing through the foam. Ivan rode across the ocean on the shoulders of the Sea King. But by the time they reached the harbour, the church bells were already ringing. Ivan's eldest brother was about to marry the Tsarevna. Chudo Yudo placed Ivan on the shore.

"Ivan, promise me one thing," he said. "Never boast about riding on my shoulders. If you do, I will hear you and destroy you."

Ivan bowed and promised not to tell a soul.

Then he ran to the church. The wedding march was playing, and the Tsarevna was walking down the aisle looking very sad indeed. But when she saw Ivan, she threw back her veil and cried, "That's the true bridegroom over there."

Everyone turned and looked at Ivan. And Ivan's father leapt to his feet.

"Your brothers told me that you'd fallen overboard and drowned," he said, wiping away his tears. "Oh, how happy I am to see you again!"

"I did not fall, Father," said Ivan. And he told all about the salt, the gold, the Tsar's daughter and his brothers throwing him overboard. At once the congregation began to shout,

"Kill those evil brothers!"

"Put them in a bottomless boat!"

"Push them out to sea!"

But Ivan took both his brothers by the hand and said softly, "No. I understand exactly why you wanted to drown me, and I forgive you. If you should die now, then this whole adventure would have been for nothing."

Then Ivan turned to the congregation and said, "Let the real wedding begin!"

So Ivan married the Tsarevna. And there was a huge wedding party, with eating, dancing, singing, and storytelling. But most of all, drinking vodka! Ivan went back to his old ways. He drank, the sea dogs drank, and they all told jokes and boasted. They boasted about how their ship was the finest, their horse the fastest and their daughter the cleverest. Then Ivan shouted at the top of his voice, "But I'm the only one in the whole wide world who has ridden on the shoulders of the Sea King!"

Hardly had the words slipped out of his mouth, when there was a rumbling and a bubbling and the ground began to shake. A huge wave crashed on to the shore and Chudo Yudo, the King of the Sea, burst into the hall.

"I heard you boasting, Ivan," he roared, "and I told you what would

happen if you did."

"Your Majesty," trembled Ivan. "Forgive me. It wasn't me boasting, it was the vodka!"

"What?" blazed the Sea King. "How can vodka boast?"

"I will show you," cried Ivan.

The old sea dogs rolled a barrel of vodka across the floor and tapped a hole in the top.

"Try it," said Ivan.

Chudo Yudo picked up the barrel, as if it was a drinking glass, and took a gulp.

"Mmmm, nice!" he grunted, and glugged down the whole barrel!

"Ecshellent... dilishussss..." he giggled.

The Sea King roared with laughter and staggered round the hall. He was drunk! He tumbled to the ground and rolled from side to side. He lashed his tentacles wildly and crushed all the feasting tables. The wedding guests scattered and Chudo Yudo flattened the whole hall. He uprooted trees, destroyed fields and smashed houses. Until, at last, he fell asleep. The Sea King slept for three days, and when he finally awoke

he had a terrible headache!

"What has happened?" he moaned, staring at the devastation. "There must have been a terrible storm."

"A storm didn't do this," laughed Ivan. "You did!"

"It wasn't me who made this mess," bellowed the Sea King. "It was the vodka! And if vodka can do that much damage, then a little bit of boasting doesn't really matter at all. You can boast about me for the next thousand years if you like!"

And Chudo Yudo stumbled into the sea and sank down under the waves.

Ivan looked at the damage and thought, "My brothers were right to want to drown me. I was drowning myself in all that vodka."

And he vowed never to touch another drop of vodka for the rest of his life. His brothers were very pleased about this. And they were even happier when Ivan repaired all the damage and built them each a new house.

Ivan and the Tsarevna lived a long and happy life. But Ivan did not give up boasting, the Sea King's boast lives on. For he told this tale to somebody, who told it to somebody, who told it to somebody, who told it to me. And as I have just told it to you, what do you have to do?

THE WHALE
WHO MADE
THE TIDES

EAST AFRICA

Into the vast endless ocean of the universe swam Chewa the giant whale. Chewa was colossal. He was so enormous that on his back there stood a mountain. And on the mountain stood a cow. And between the cow's long horns was the world, our world, gently balanced.

Chewa swam slowly through the dark ocean of space, carrying the world on his back. He swam carefully, so he would not tip the world. He swam so carefully that not one drop of water on earth moved. Chewa swam back and forth, through the glittering stars, for hundreds and hundreds of generations.

Then one day, Chewa heard that his father had died. Chewa was sad, but he did not complain. He continued to swim back and forth through the ocean of space.

Then Chewa heard that his mother had died. Chewa was very sad, but he still did not complain. He just carried on swimming.

And then, Chewa heard that his wife had died. When Chewa heard that, he was so very sad, he opened his giant mouth and a terrible cry came out.

Chewa's cry echoed throughout the whole universe. He cried and cried and cried. The giant heart in his giant body broke in two. His cries got louder and louder and his mouth got wider and wider. Chewa quite forgot about the world on his back, and he rolled over in the ocean of space, over on to his side. And as he rolled, the rock on his back rolled. And as the rock on his back rolled, the cow on the rock rolled. And as the cow on the rock rolled, the world balanced between the cow's horns rolled. And as the world balanced between the cow's horns rolled, all the water on earth tipped to one side and was washed up on the shore. The people living on earth had never seen anything like that before, and they called it – HIGH TIDE!

Then Chewa rolled over on to his other side. And as he rolled, the rock on his back rolled, and the cow on the rock rolled, and the world between the cow's horns rolled. And all the water on earth was washed away from the shore.

The people on earth had never seen anything like that before, and they called it – LOW TIDE!

And do you know what – Chewa is still crying!

And that is why we have the tides today.

Spell to Make your Ship Go

Sail my red vessel
Splash oars through water
Run along the billows
Fly over the ocean

Charm from Ancient Finland

CHURNING
THE
MILKY OCEAN

When time began, the Gods and the Demons lived on earth together.
The Gods protected the earth, but the Demons destroyed it. The
Demons plagued the world, and the Gods gradually lost their power.
They grew weak and old, their hair turned white and their teeth fell out.
As the Gods lost their power, so the earth perished. There were floods,
famines and diseases. The earth was on the brink of being overrun by
Demons.

In desperation, the Gods went to see Vishnu, the great Sun God who
keeps everything alive. The frail Gods shuffled along the seashore until
they found Vishnu. He was floating in the ocean, resting on the
thousand-headed serpent, Vasuki. The Sun God shone with light, he
was full of health and strength.

"O Lord Vishnu, Maintainer of Life!" cried the Gods. "We need
your help. The Demons are overwhelming the world and we have lost
all our power."

Vishnu opened his eyes and gazed at the old and trembling Gods.

"There is only one way for you to regain your strength and overcome
the demons!" he murmured. "You must churn the ocean, as if you were

churning milk to make butter. Churn the ocean for the cream of life – the ambrosia of immortality. One sip of the ambrosia will renew your strength for ever more."

"We will never be able to churn the ocean!" sighed the Gods. "We are getting weaker by the minute."

"Ask the Demons for help," replied Vishnu. "Offer them half the ambrosia of immortality. But do not fear. I will make sure that for their labour they will have all pain and no gain!"

So the Gods entered into a pact with the Demons, promising them half the ambrosia of immortality. Together they pulled up Mount Mandara by the roots. They turned the mighty mountain upside down and stood it in the sea. This would be their churning stick. Then they called on Vasuki, the thousand-headed serpent, and they wrapped him round the mountain three times. He would be their churning rope.

Then the Gods took hold of the serpent by his thousand heads, and they gave the Demons the serpent's tail. The Demons were not happy with this.

"It's not fair," they snarled. "Why should you have a thousand heads while we only get one tail? We want the heads!"

"Very well," said the Gods, "you take the heads and we'll have the tail."

So the Gods pulled the serpent's tail one way, and the Demons pulled the serpent's heads the other way. As they pulled the serpent back and forth, the mountain began to twirl. And as the mountain twirled, the sea began to churn. The ocean was whipped up into white crested waves. The Gods and Demons pulled Vasuki faster and faster and faster. The sea frothed and foamed. They pulled the serpent so fast that he got hot, boiling hot. Flames shot out of his thousand mouths, singeing and scorching the Demons. While fresh breezes blew from his tail, fanning the Gods and keeping them cool!

The mountain twirled so fast that it bored a hole down into the sandy ocean bed and began to sink! Vishnu was watching, and he instantly turned himself into a turtle and plunged to the bottom of the sea. He heaved the massive mountain out of the sand and placed it on top of his curved back. The tip of Mount Mandara rested on his unbreakable shell. His turtle shell became a pivot and the mountain whirled

away smoothly. The mountain turned and the ocean churned. The
ocean turned to milk, and the treasures of the milky ocean appeared.

First came the slender shining silver moon. It floated on the surface
of the sea. The God of Dance, Lord Shiva, plucked the moon out of the
ocean and fixed it in his black hair. The moon still shines in Shiva's hair
making the ocean rise and fall with the tides.

Next came the beautiful Goddess Lakshmi, sitting on a lotus flower.
The Mother of All Living Things, who ripens the harvest and brings
abundance.

Then came two elephants, white as clouds, who showered soft water
over Lakshmi's head in blessing.

Then came the wish-fulfilling cow, Surabhi, who grants wishes from
the everlasting milk that flows from her udders.

Then came the paradise tree, Parijata. A delicate tree covered in
blossom, whose fragrance fills the world.

As each treasure rose to the surface, the Gods gasped in wonder. But the Demons were only interested in the ambrosia of immortality, and they pulled the serpent ever faster.

Vasuki got hotter and hotter, until a lump of black poison rose up into his throat. The poison was so strong that just one drop would have destroyed the whole world. At once Shiva ran to Vasuki's thousand heads. Vasuki opened his thousand mouths and vomited out the lump of poison. But Shiva quickly caught the poison in his mouth. Not a single drop touched the earth.

Shiva's wife, Parvati, was horrified! If Shiva swallowed the poison, he would be destroyed. So Parvati clasped her hands around Shiva's throat and choked him! The poison stayed in his throat. Shiva did not swallow it. But his throat turned blue. And his throat has been blue ever since. For Shiva still holds the poison in his throat, to protect the world, to this very day.

At last, the milky ocean began to thicken. The mountain slowed down, the mountain stopped. The milk had turned to cream. Out of the creamy ocean rose an old, old man, dressed

in white and carrying a golden goblet. It was the wise physician with the ambrosia of immortality.

The Gods stood transfixed, staring at the cup in silence. Suddenly there was a roar like thunder, and the Demons leapt forward, grabbed the goblet and disappeared.

The Demons carried the ambrosia of immortality down to hell. But as soon as they arrived, they began to argue about who should have the first sip! The Demons pulled the cup this way and that, shrieking and screaming – they just could not decide.

When, into hell, walked a woman they had never seen before. Her bracelets and anklets tinkled, she had long dark hair, shining eyes and a rosy mouth. She was ravishingly beautiful. The Demons stared, mesmerised by her beauty. They forgot all about the golden goblet.

"Who is she?" they chattered.

"No human or God could be so exquisite. She must be a demon!"

"Don't you recognise me?" smiled the woman. "I am Mohini. I am your desire!" And she flashed her eyes.

The Demons were swept into a frenzy of passion. They crowded round Mohini crying, "Let Mohini decide who should have the first sip!"

"Surely," charmed Mohini in a sugar-sweet voice, "you can't trust a mere woman with such an important decision?"

The Demons went wild with rapture, they were spellbound.

"Let Mohini decide!" they chanted.

"Very well," agreed Mohini, "I will decide. But you must abide by my decision."

The Demons nodded and pressed even closer.

"You churned the ocean," said Mohini, "but you did not churn it

alone. The Gods must have their half of the ambrosia."

So the Gods were summoned to hell. Mohini lined them up in two
long lines facing each other, the Gods on one side and the Demons on
the other. Then she picked up the golden goblet. Mohini walked slowly
down the line of Gods, lifting the goblet to their ancient trembling lips.
As they sipped the ambrosia of immortality, their backs straightened,
their hair turned thick and dark. They were filled with youth and
strength. When Mohini reached the end of the line, she turned to the
Demons – and vanished! With her vanished the golden goblet and the
ambrosia of immortality. Mohini did not exist. Mohini was just an
illusion. She was Vishnu in disguise! The Demons had been tricked by
their own desire.

The Demons were filled with rage. They waged war on the Gods,
hurling mountains and showering plagues. But the battle did not last

long. For the Gods had regained all their power. Vishnu spun his silver discus, Shiva launched his three-pronged trident, and Demons were slaughtered by the thousand. The rest of the Demons retreated underground to hell. And there they have remained ever since!

Order was restored to the world once more. Then the Gods walked to the seashore to thank Vishnu. The great Sun God was already resting on the thousand-headed serpent. And he was just about to close his eyes and fall asleep, to dream the dream of the world.

The Gods bowed low before him.

"Lord of all, Maintainer of Life, how can we ever thank you?" they begged.

"Give me the Goddess Lakshmi as my wife," he replied. For even Vishnu could not resist his desire.

And so Vishnu married the beautiful Goddess Lakshmi. And whenever Vishnu wakes from his sleep, to help those in trouble, Lakshmi is always beside him.

Since that time, the Gods have had immortal life. And as for us — there is no immortality. But it is said that those who have sipped on this story will be revived and blessed for the rest of their lives.

THE
FIVE MAGIC
BROTHERS

CHINA

Once there were five brothers who all looked exactly the same. They had been born on the same day and were identical quins. No one could tell the difference between them, except for their old mother. But even though they looked the same, they were very different, for each brother had his own special magical power.

The first brother could swallow the sea. The second brother had an iron neck. The third brother could not be burned. The fourth brother could hold his breath for as long as he liked. And the fifth brother could stretch his legs until one foot was in China and the other foot was in England!

The five brothers lived with their old mother in a bamboo hut on the shores of the South China Sea. Every morning the first brother would go down to the beach to fish. He would put his lips to the water, and suck and suck and suck up the whole sea. Then he would fill his pail with fish stranded on the sand, spit the sea back out again and take the fish home for lunch!

One day a little boy asked the first brother to take him fishing. The boy begged and pleaded so much that in the end the first brother agreed.

"But the kind of fishing I do," warned the first brother, "is very dangerous. When I wave to you, you must come and stand beside me straight away. Do you understand?"

"Yes, sir!" said the boy happily.

So, early next morning, they went down to the beach together. The first brother put his lips to the water, and sucked and sucked and sucked up the whole sea. The little boy blinked his eyes in amazement for there spread out before him, was the invisible underwater world of the ocean bed. There were glittering shells and wrecked ships, seaweed trees and skeletons, flapping fish and treasure chests and there was an old ship's lantern that was still alight!

The first brother began to fill his pail with fish. But the little boy was no longer interested in fishing. He was racing over the ocean bed, stuffing his pockets with shells and coins. He was scrambling over a wrecked ship and digging up a rusty old box. The sea began to bubble inside the first brother's tummy. So he raised one arm, and beckoned for the boy to come and stand beside him.

"Ohh!" groaned the boy. "I won't be a moment. I've found a lovely shell."

The sea rumbled and tumbled and surged up into the first brother's mouth. He waved both his arms wildly at the boy.

"Hang on a minute," cried the boy. "I just have to look inside this barrel!"

But the first brother could not hold the sea back for a second more. He opened his mouth, and with a great rush the sea gushed out. It poured over the ocean bed and everything was covered in brimming water, everything, including the little boy.

The first brother walked sadly to the little boy's house. He told the little boy's mother all that had happened. The little boy's mother was very upset and angry.

"You killed my boy!" she shouted. "You will be punished."

And she marched the first brother straight to the High Court. The mother told her story and the first brother told his. The Judge listened and shook his head gravely.

"This man is a criminal and deserves to die," he proclaimed. "Tomorrow his head will be chopped from his body. But, as is the tradition in this country, he may have one last request."

"Please can I go and say goodbye to my old mother?" asked the first brother.

"Very well," nodded the Judge. "But come back tomorrow."

The first brother went home and told his mother and his four brothers the whole story. "And tomorrow," he finished, "my head is going to be chopped from my body."

When the second brother heard that he had a brilliant idea.

"We all look exactly the same," he grinned. "Why don't I go instead of you? The Judge will never know the difference!"

So, the next morning, the second brother bowed before the Judge.

"Ah, good! The criminal has returned," said the Judge, rubbing his hands. "Now, put your head on the block."

The second brother knelt down and placed his head on the executioner's block.

The Judge lifted a shining silver sword high above his head and brought it slicing through the air straight on to the second brother's neck. But the head did not roll cleanly away from the body as it usually did. The sword clanged on to the iron neck and bent.

"Oh bother!" grumbled the Judge. "I thought this sword was getting old."

He called for a brand-new sword with a very sharp edge. He raised the sword with a flourish and brought it swiftly down. The sword clanged on to the iron neck and snapped in two! The Judge was furious. He pulled out his little pocket dagger and began sawing away at the second brother's neck.

"Your neck's as tough as old iron!" he grunted.

The second brother smiled. The Judge's dagger was soon blunt!

"Right," ordered the Judge. "I cannot chop your head off, so tomorrow I will burn you alive. But you may have one last request."

"Please can I go and say goodbye to my old mother?" asked the second brother.

So the second brother went home, and the next morning the third brother came back! "Stand on top of this pile of sticks," said the Judge. The third brother climbed on to a huge bonfire of sticks and the Judge tied his hands behind his back. Then the Judge took a burning fiery brand and lit the bonfire. Flames began to crackle and blaze all around the third brother.

"Oohh!" shuddered the third brother, "it's a little chilly in here, could you get some more sticks please?"

The Judge could not believe his ears. He threw a large tree on to the fire. The tree burnt red-hot and the flames licked up the third brother's legs. But he stood in the middle of the fire, smiling,

"That's better! Nice and warm – just how I like it!"

"Right," ordered the Judge. "I cannot burn you, so tomorrow I will bury you. But you may have one last request."

"Please can I go and say goodbye to my old mother?" asked the third brother.

So the third brother went home, and the next morning the fourth brother came back.

"Climb into this hole," said the Judge.

The fourth brother jumped into a deep hole. He lay down, made himself comfortable, breathed in and held his breath.

The Judge took a spade and filled the hole up with earth, so that the fourth brother was completely buried. Then the Judge sat down beside the mound of earth and waited. The moon rose and the moon set. The sun rose and the sun set.

The moon rose and...the Judge waited until three days had passed.

"The criminal is dead at last," he announced. "I will now dig him up, and his mother can give him a proper funeral."

The Judge took his spade and dug away all the earth. At the bottom of the hole, the fourth brother breathed out.

"Aahh!" he sighed. "That was a nice sleep."

The Judge could not believe his eyes.

"HELP!" he screamed. "It's a ghost!"

The fourth brother stood up, stretched, yawned and brushed the earth from his clothes.

"I am certainly not a ghost," he smiled.

"RIGHT!" thundered the Judge. "I can not bury you, so tomorrow I will drown you. And, yes, you can go and say goodbye to your old mother first!"

So the fourth brother went home, and the next morning, the fifth brother came back.

"Get into this boat!" said the Judge.

The fifth brother stepped into the boat and was rowed far out to the deepest part of the sea. Then the Judge picked him up and dropped him over the side of the boat.

"Good riddance!" said the Judge, breathing a sigh of relief.

But the fifth brother stretched and stretched and stretched his legs, until he was standing on the sandy ocean bed. The fish swam around his kneecaps, his head bobbed about on the surface of the sea, and the seagulls swooped down and pecked at his nose!

Suddenly the fifth brother heard a tiny cry:

"Help! I'm in here!"

The sound was coming from a wooden barrel floating on the waves. Inside there was a little boy, who was wet and bedraggled and very scared.

"Help! I'm in here!" he sobbed.

The fifth brother took the little boy into his arms.

"Ahoy!" he called. "Ship ahoy! I've found the little boy!"

The Judge rowed the boat alongside the barrel and lifted the boy safely on board. The fifth brother just had time to shrink his legs back to their normal size, before the Judge pulled him out of the sea too. As soon as the fifth brother was on the deck, the Judge fell on his knees before him.

"I have made a terrible mistake," pleaded the Judge. "You were innocent all along. That is why the sword would not cut you. Why the fire would not burn you. Why the earth would not bury you. And why the water would not drown you. Will you ever forgive me?"

The fifth brother smiled and said nothing!

When they reached the shore, the fifth brother carried the little boy

all the way home. The little boy's mother was so happy to see her son she hugged him very tightly. So tightly that she felt all the lumps and bumps in his stuffed full pockets.

"What have you got in your pockets?" she asked.

The boy emptied his pockets, and out tumbled piles of pirate gold.

"Now," said the boy's mother sternly, "you give all that gold to this kind man, who has had nothing but trouble because of you, and who has saved your life."

The fifth brother went home laden with gold. And the five brothers and their old mother laughed and laughed and laughed. As for the Judge, well he *still* thinks that the old mother has only got one son! But as for you, well, you know the true story.

Rolling Home

Three wise men of Gotham
Went to sea in a bowl.
If that bowl had been stronger
My tale would have been longer!

Old English Nonsense Verse

93

THE
MONKEY
AND THE
FOOLISH JELLYFISH

JAPAN

A long time ago, down at the bottom of the deepest sea, lived the Dragon King and Queen. They had a palace made of red and white coral, and they were waited on tooth and claw by a stream of sea-creature servants. The royal dragons wanted for nothing.

Then one day the Dragon Queen fell sick. She lay on her jewelled couch and would not get up. So the royal doctor was called. He could not find anything wrong with the Queen. He gave her pills and potions, hot baths and lotions. But the Dragon Queen just got sicker and paler, limper and frailer, until the Dragon King was afraid that she might die.

"My own true and fiery love," he begged. "Is there nothing that will make you well?"

"Yes," whispered the Queen weakly. "There is one thing."

"Tell me, my darling," said the King, stroking his wife's scaley brow. "Whatever it is, you must have it."

"If only I could eat a monkey's liver," replied the Queen, "I should get well at once."

"A monkey's liver!" exclaimed the King. "But that is impossible. Monkeys live in the tops of trees, and we live at the bottom of the sea."

"Well," sighed the Queen, "if I don't get a monkey's liver, I will die."

So the King hastily called for his faithful servant, the Jellyfish. In those days jellyfish were rather different from how they are now. They had the most beautiful pearly shells that completely covered their bodies. The faithful Jellyfish bowed before the King.

"Jellyfish," said the King, "you and you alone, have been chosen to fetch the one thing that will save the Queen's life. Swim up to the shallow waters and bring me a monkey's liver."

"B...b...but..." blustered the Jellyfish.

"Bring me the liver by sunset!" ordered the King.

So the Jellyfish set off. He floated up through the dark green waters, through the deep blue waters and into the silver sunlit waters surrounding a little island. On the shore was a tall tree and sitting in the treetop was a monkey eating a banana.

"I'm in luck!" said the Jellyfish to himself. "I just have to get him out of the tree and on to my back."

"O Monkey!" called the Jellyfish.
"O magnificent and marvellous Monkey!
At last I have found you!"

The Monkey stopped eating his banana and peered down at the Jellyfish.

"Who are you?" he chattered.

"I am the faithful servant of the great Dragon King," replied the Jellyfish grandly. "And I have crossed the whole ocean looking for you. His Majesty, the Dragon King, is lying on his death bed. He has decreed that there is only one person important enough to be King after him and sit upon his throne, and that, dear Monkey – is you!"

"ME?" squealed the Monkey.

"Yes, Sir Monkey, you! Now climb on my back and I will take you to the throne at once!"

Monkey shot down the tree and clambered on to the Jellyfish's shell. It was smooth and round and very comfortable. Monkey held on tight and Jellyfish set off over the waves. When they were far out to sea, the Jellyfish began to snigger.

"You don't really think that you, a mere monkey, are going to be

King? Oh no! I am
taking you to the palace
of the Dragon King
because his wife is sick.
And she will only get
better if she eats a
monkey's liver."

Monkey's heart raced with
terror. But his brain worked pretty
fast as well, and he said, "Why didn't
you tell me before? You see, I haven't got
my liver with me."

"What!" gasped the Jellyfish. "You mean you
go about without your liver?"

"You don't know much about monkeys, do you?
We monkeys have big livers - that is probably why
your queen wants to eat one. During the day we
take our livers out and hang them up in a tree so
that we can run about and play. Then at night we
put our livers back in so that we can go to sleep. If
only you had told me what you wanted, I would
have brought my liver with me."

"Oh dear, oh dear, oh dear," blubbed the
Jellyfish. "What am I going to do? The King
wants the liver by sunset."

"Never mind," soothed Monkey. "If you turn round now and swim back to the island, I can pick up my liver and we will still be at the palace by sunset."

So the Jellyfish turned round and swam back to the island as fast as he could. As soon as they reached the shore, the Monkey sprang off the Jellyfish's back and raced up a tree. Then he began searching among the branches.

"It doesn't seem to be here," he muttered.

Monkey rustled the leaves.

"I can't find my liver here either."

Monkey scrabbled around at the roots.

"No. My liver is nowhere to be seen. I must have mislaid it, or maybe someone has borrowed it. If you could come back tomorrow, I am sure I will have found it by then."

Jellyfish was very disappointed and he swam out to sea without the liver. But Monkey sat safely on top of the tall tree and watched him go, chuckling to himself and eating a banana.

Jellyfish floated down through the deep blue water, into the dark green water, to the bottom of the sea, and bowed before the Dragon King.

"I am terribly sorry, Your Majesty," he trembled. "Monkey did not have his liver with him. But he said if I come back tomorrow he will be sure to have found it by then."

When the Dragon King heard that, his eyes lit up and black smoke blazed from his nostrils.

"Oh, you foolish Jellyfish! Have you ever heard of any creature going about without its liver?" he roared. "I'll tell you where that monkey's liver was, it was right there inside his body, all along!"

The Dragon King was filled with rage. He picked up his royal sceptre and brought it down – SMASH – on to Jellyfish's back. The Jellyfish's shell cracked, and out spurted all the jelly. And that is why, ever since then, jellyfish have not had shells, they have just been made of wibbly, wobbly jelly!

When the Dragon Queen heard the story, she grinned, then she giggled, then she shrieked with laughter.

"Ah!" she smiled, wiping the tears from her eyes. "Forget about the monkey's liver – bring me my best brocade gown. I am getting up. There is nothing like a good tale to make you feel better!"

HINA
AND THE
EEL OF PLENTY

MANGAIA

Far, far away, on a tiny island in the middle of the Pacific Ocean, there lived a very beautiful girl. She was called Hina, and her name meant 'nine moons'. The other people living on the island thought that Hina was the daughter of the moon. For she did not have a mother or father, and her long black hair shone with a silvery light.

Hina lived alone in a little hut on the highest part of the island. Every day she would fetch water, catch fish and scratch the ground for roots. But often there was not enough food or fresh water to go round, and people went hungry. Hina hoped that one day plenty would come to the island. Then there would be enough for everyone.

When Hina's work was done, she would walk down to the sea, to a lagoon surrounded by dazzling coral reefs. And as the sun set she would dive into the cool clear water and bathe.

One evening, while Hina was swimming, an eel slithered into the lagoon. The eel was enormous; seven feet long, thick as a rope, and an oily black colour. His skin was smooth and firm and his beady black eyes glistened. The eel circled round Hina and brushed against her legs. Hina stayed very still, for the eel could easily crush her in his strong jaws. But the eel did not harm her. He rippled his body, flicked his tail, and plunged out of sight. Suddenly there was a splash, Hina whirled round and the eel popped up behind her! Hina began to laugh – the eel wanted to play! As she swam through the cool water, the eel swooped and glided silently beside her.

Every evening after that the eel was waiting in the lagoon for Hina. They played together – diving and splashing, racing and basking – until Hina and the eel had become great friends.

Then one evening when Hina was about to go home, the eel opened his small round mouth and spoke in a human voice.

"Hina," he hissed, "I am the King of the Eels. You have been such a good friend to me, I want to give you a gift. Tomorrow, when you come to bathe, bring an axe."

Hina was amazed to hear the eel speaking, and all night she wondered what his mysterious words might mean.

The next evening Hina carried a little flint axe to the lagoon. As usual, the eel was waiting for her.

"Hina," he whispered, "if you love me, chop off my head."

Hina was horrified.

"Oh no!" she cried. "I could never do that! You are my best friend."

The eel stared hard at Hina with his beady eyes and spoke solemnly.

"Hina, if you do not chop off my head, Poverty will come to this island and you will never see my face again. But, if you are brave enough to chop off my head, Plenty will come to this island and you will see my face for ever more."

Hina began to weep. But the eel murmured, "Chop off my head, Hina. Then throw my body into the lagoon, and bury my head beside your hut."

Hina knew that she must trust the King of the Eels and do what he asked. So she bent down and kissed him goodbye. Then she held his head very gently and lifted her axe. In one swift and skilful stroke she chopped off the eel's head. She picked up the eel's lifeless body and threw it into the lagoon. Then she picked up the eel's lifeless head and

carried it carefully home. She dug a deep hole in the dry ground beside her hut. And she tenderly laid the eel's head in the bottom of the hole, covered it with fresh earth and patted it smooth.

Hina felt as if her heart would break. She was so sad, she went straight to bed. It seemed as if the whole world was sad too, for during the night it began to rain. It had not rained for many weeks, and large hard raindrops pounded on the roof of her hut all night long. In the morning, when Hina opened the door, the rain had stopped and the sun was shining. Everything smelled fresh and new.

Hina went to look at the eel's grave. And where she had buried him, peeping out of the wet earth, was a firm green shoot! Hina's heart felt a little lighter. She ran down to the lagoon, and something was darting to and fro in the water. The lagoon was teeming with tiny, silver baby eels!

Hina's heart felt much lighter!

Every day Hina tended the green shoot and it began to grow. And as the shoot grew, the baby eels grew! The tiny shoot grew until it had become a tall, slender graceful tree with broad spreading leaves. The eels grew until they were big enough to swim out of the lagoon and away into the blue sea.

All the islanders came to look at Hina's tree. They had never seen such a tall tree, and its feathery leaves gave a lovely cool shade. Right at the top of the tree, a fruit began to grow. It was round and hard. The fruit grew and grew. Until one day a boy clambered up the tree, picked the fruit and gave it to Hina. It was heavy and Hina turned it over in her hands.

"Is this Plenty?" she wondered.

Hina took her axe and sliced open the fruit. Inside there was a large nut surrounded by bristly hair. Hina sliced open the nut shell. Inside there was sweet fresh milk to drink and juicy white flesh to eat!

Every part of the nut could be used. The juicy flesh could be pressed to make oil for anointing hair and skin. The hard shell could be made into cups and bowls and ladles. The bristly hair could be twisted into ropes and baskets. The sap of the tree could be made into palm wine. The broad leaves could be woven into mats. And the dead wood from the tree could be used to build huts and canoes.

Plenty *had* come to the island. There was plenty for everyone! People would never be hungry again. Hina turned the precious nut over in her hands. Suddenly she saw something strange on the bottom of its shell. It was a face. It had two beady black eyes and a small round mouth. It was the face of the King of the Eels! And he was smiling. Hina's heart filled with happiness. Everything the King of the Eels had said had come true. Hina would see the eel's face for ever more!

The islanders still call the juicy white flesh of the nut 'eel's brains'! And when the moon is full and the tide is right, the eel's many children swim back to the lagoon. But as for his face, well, it is still there. If you would like to see the face of the King of the Eels, then just look at the bottom of a coconut!

Dropping Anchor

I found the path
and you found the puddle.
I was drowned
and you were found.
If it's all one to you today,
it won't be all one to you the next day.
And if it wasn't for the stories,
you'd have nothing to lose
but an old back tooth!

Old Irish saying

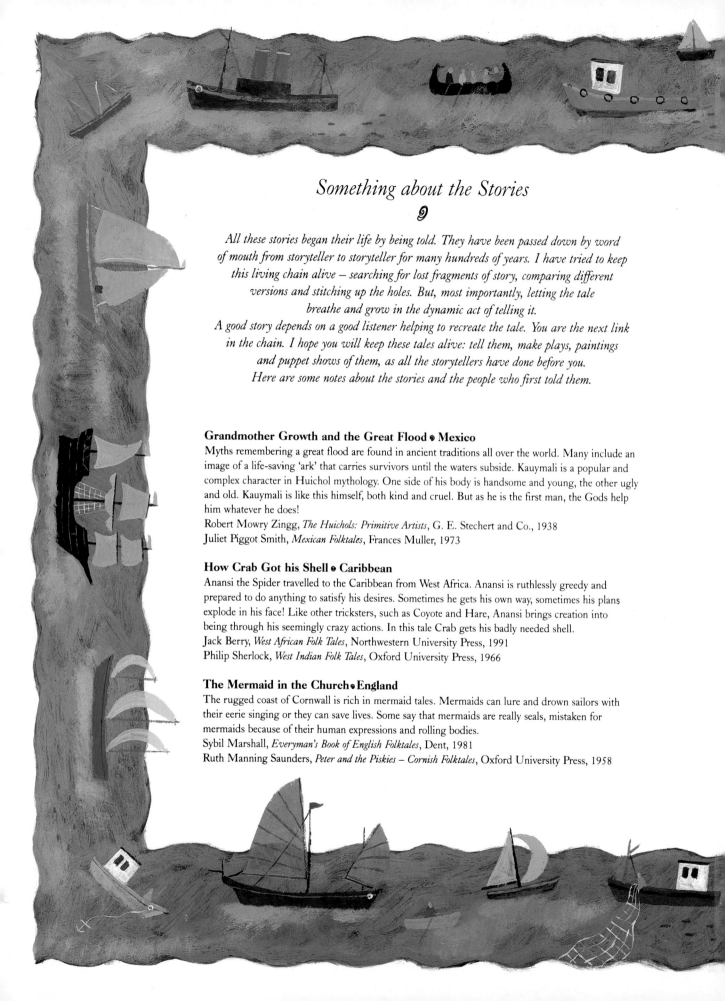

Something about the Stories

All these stories began their life by being told. They have been passed down by word of mouth from storyteller to storyteller for many hundreds of years. I have tried to keep this living chain alive – searching for lost fragments of story, comparing different versions and stitching up the holes. But, most importantly, letting the tale breathe and grow in the dynamic act of telling it.

A good story depends on a good listener helping to recreate the tale. You are the next link in the chain. I hope you will keep these tales alive: tell them, make plays, paintings and puppet shows of them, as all the storytellers have done before you. Here are some notes about the stories and the people who first told them.

Grandmother Growth and the Great Flood • Mexico

Myths remembering a great flood are found in ancient traditions all over the world. Many include an image of a life-saving 'ark' that carries survivors until the waters subside. Kauymali is a popular and complex character in Huichol mythology. One side of his body is handsome and young, the other ugly and old. Kauymali is like this himself, both kind and cruel. But as he is the first man, the Gods help him whatever he does!

Robert Mowry Zingg, *The Huichols: Primitive Artists*, G. E. Stechert and Co., 1938
Juliet Piggot Smith, *Mexican Folktales*, Frances Muller, 1973

How Crab Got his Shell • Caribbean

Anansi the Spider travelled to the Caribbean from West Africa. Anansi is ruthlessly greedy and prepared to do anything to satisfy his desires. Sometimes he gets his own way, sometimes his plans explode in his face! Like other tricksters, such as Coyote and Hare, Anansi brings creation into being through his seemingly crazy actions. In this tale Crab gets his badly needed shell.

Jack Berry, *West African Folk Tales*, Northwestern University Press, 1991
Philip Sherlock, *West Indian Folk Tales*, Oxford University Press, 1966

The Mermaid in the Church • England

The rugged coast of Cornwall is rich in mermaid tales. Mermaids can lure and drown sailors with their eerie singing or they can save lives. Some say that mermaids are really seals, mistaken for mermaids because of their human expressions and rolling bodies.

Sybil Marshall, *Everyman's Book of English Folktales*, Dent, 1981
Ruth Manning Saunders, *Peter and the Piskies – Cornish Folktales*, Oxford University Press, 1958

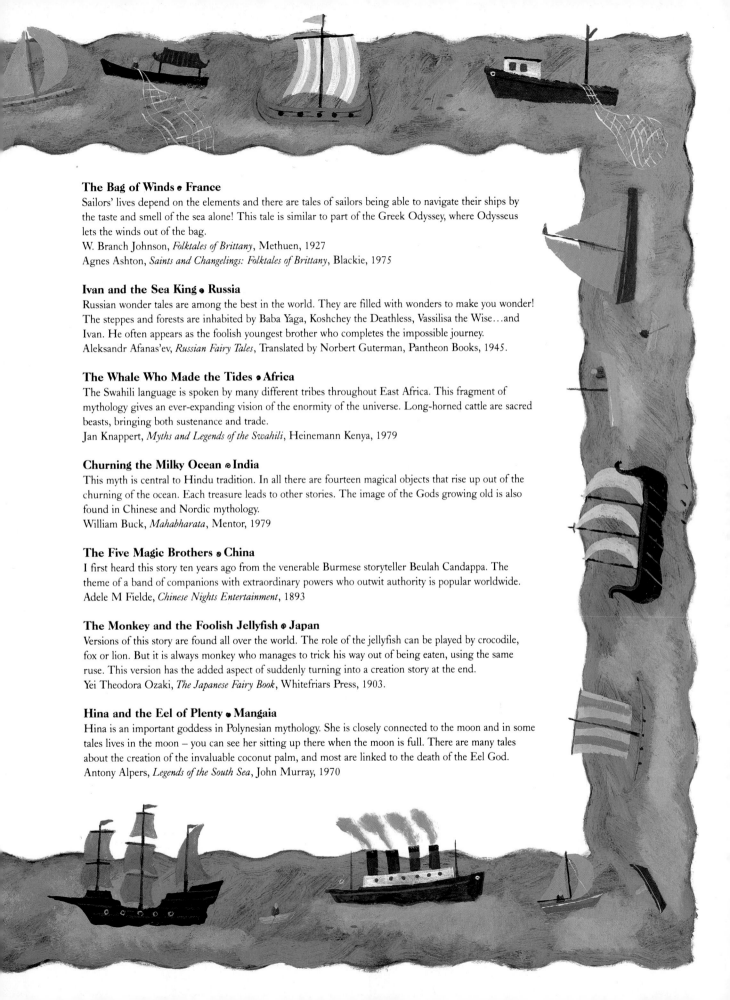

The Bag of Winds • France

Sailors' lives depend on the elements and there are tales of sailors being able to navigate their ships by the taste and smell of the sea alone! This tale is similar to part of the Greek Odyssey, where Odysseus lets the winds out of the bag.

W. Branch Johnson, *Folktales of Brittany*, Methuen, 1927

Agnes Ashton, *Saints and Changelings: Folktales of Brittany*, Blackie, 1975

Ivan and the Sea King • Russia

Russian wonder tales are among the best in the world. They are filled with wonders to make you wonder! The steppes and forests are inhabited by Baba Yaga, Koshchey the Deathless, Vassilisa the Wise…and Ivan. He often appears as the foolish youngest brother who completes the impossible journey.

Aleksandr Afanas'ev, *Russian Fairy Tales*, Translated by Norbert Guterman, Pantheon Books, 1945.

The Whale Who Made the Tides • Africa

The Swahili language is spoken by many different tribes throughout East Africa. This fragment of mythology gives an ever-expanding vision of the enormity of the universe. Long-horned cattle are sacred beasts, bringing both sustenance and trade.

Jan Knappert, *Myths and Legends of the Swahili*, Heinemann Kenya, 1979

Churning the Milky Ocean • India

This myth is central to Hindu tradition. In all there are fourteen magical objects that rise up out of the churning of the ocean. Each treasure leads to other stories. The image of the Gods growing old is also found in Chinese and Nordic mythology.

William Buck, *Mahabharata*, Mentor, 1979

The Five Magic Brothers • China

I first heard this story ten years ago from the venerable Burmese storyteller Beulah Candappa. The theme of a band of companions with extraordinary powers who outwit authority is popular worldwide.

Adele M Fielde, *Chinese Nights Entertainment*, 1893

The Monkey and the Foolish Jellyfish • Japan

Versions of this story are found all over the world. The role of the jellyfish can be played by crocodile, fox or lion. But it is always monkey who manages to trick his way out of being eaten, using the same ruse. This version has the added aspect of suddenly turning into a creation story at the end.

Yei Theodora Ozaki, *The Japanese Fairy Book*, Whitefriars Press, 1903.

Hina and the Eel of Plenty • Mangaia

Hina is an important goddess in Polynesian mythology. She is closely connected to the moon and in some tales lives in the moon – you can see her sitting up there when the moon is full. There are many tales about the creation of the invaluable coconut palm, and most are linked to the death of the Eel God.

Antony Alpers, *Legends of the South Sea*, John Murray, 1970

NORTH PACIFIC OCEAN

NORTH ATLANTIC OCEAN

SOUTH PACIFIC OCEAN

SOUTH ATLANTIC OCEAN

WO

A
O